This edition published by Parragon Books Ltd in 2016 and distributed by

Parragon Inc.
440 Park Avenue South, 13th Floor
New York, NY 10016
www.parragon.com

Copyright © Parragon Books Ltd 2016

Retold by Rachel Elliot   Illustrated by John Joven
Edited by Grace Harvey   Designed by Karissa Santos and Duck Egg Blue
Production by Danielle Nevin

ISBN 978-1-4748-6043-7

Printed in China

JOSEPH AND HIS COAT OF MANY COLORS

Bath • New York • Cologne • Melbourne • Delhi
Hong Kong • Shenzhen • Singapore

Of Jacob's twelve sons, Joseph was his favorite. Joseph was kind and helpful, and his mother Rachel had been Jacob's most beloved wife. She had died, and Jacob missed her very much, but Joseph reminded him of her every day.

Jacob's ten eldest sons were too busy to spend much time with him, and his youngest son Benjamin was too young, but Joseph, the second youngest, loved sitting and talking with his father. They were good friends as well as being father and son.

Jacob enjoyed showing Joseph how much he was loved. He bought him a special coat, woven in bright, beautiful colors, to keep him warm while he and his older brothers tended the sheep on the hills.

"Thank you, Father," said Joseph, hugging Jacob. "I love it!"

Joseph's brothers felt jealous, because Joseph was their father's favorite. They had only plain, threadbare jackets, so when they saw Joseph's new coat, they disliked him even more.

One day, the brothers were walking home from the hills to help harvest the fields in Canaan, where they lived. Joseph's brothers were ignoring him and muttering mean things about him. But Joseph didn't notice that they were being unkind, because he was thinking about a dream he had had the night before.

"I had a dream about the harvest last night," he said. "We each had a sheaf of golden corn standing in the field. Mine stood tall, while your smaller sheaves bowed down to it. I think it's a message from God. What do you think it means?"

His brothers were furious.

"Do you think you're better than us?" they asked.

Joseph felt terrible. He wanted his brothers to love him, but telling them about his dream had made them hate him even more.

A short time later, Joseph had another dream that he couldn't understand. He decided to tell his father and his brothers about it when they were all together at home. Perhaps his father would know what it meant.

"I had another dream last night," Joseph said one evening, trying to ignore the angry looks from his brothers. "This time, the Sun and Moon and eleven stars in the glittering night sky were bowing down to me. What could it mean?"

His brothers were enraged, and even his father frowned.

"Do you think that your brothers and I will come and bow down to you?" Jacob asked.

Joseph didn't dare to say any more, and Jacob didn't mention it again, but he didn't forget about Joseph's strange dream.

Over time, Joseph's brothers grew more and more jealous of Joseph. They left him out of everything and wanted to make him suffer for being their father's favorite.

One day, when the older brothers were out looking after the sheep and Benjamin was at home, Jacob sent Joseph to find out how they were doing. When the older brothers saw Joseph coming in his colorful coat, all their hateful feelings bubbled up.

"I've had enough of this dreamer," one brother snarled.

"If only we could get rid of him," said another.

"We could do what we liked to him out here," said a third. "We could say it was a wild animal. He might even die."

The others felt such hatred toward Joseph that hurting him suddenly didn't seem like such a bad thing to do. Only Reuben, Joseph's eldest brother, tried to stop them.

"Let's not kill him. Just throw him into a dry well," he said, thinking that he could rescue Joseph later when the others had calmed down.

The other brothers ripped Joseph's beautiful coat from his back and threw him into a dry well. But, while Reuben was tending to the sheep, they saw a group of travelers, called Ishmaelites, coming their way.

Another brother, Judah, had an idea. "We won't gain anything from killing Joseph," he said. "Let's sell him!"

So the greedy brothers sold Joseph for twenty pieces of silver. Shocked and hurt, Joseph was carried far away.

Reuben was horrified when he found out what his brothers had done. "How can we explain this to our father?" he cried.

"We'll make it sound like an accident," said Judah.

The brothers dipped Joseph's coat in animal blood, so it looked as if a wild beast had eaten him. Then, they took it home to Jacob. Believing that his dearest son was dead, Jacob's heart broke into pieces.

"I will go to my grave mourning for my son," he said.

Joseph was taken far away to Egypt. He was sold as a slave to a man named Potiphar. Potiphar was an important man who worked for Pharaoh, who was in charge of all Egypt.

"I am now a slave," Joseph said to himself. "It must be God's plan for me."

At first, Joseph's life in Egypt was not too bad. Joseph knew that God would want him to do his best. He worked hard and soon became an important servant. God blessed Potiphar's house, because Joseph was there.

His master Potiphar trusted him and everyone liked him—everyone except Potiphar's wife. Filled with wickedness and jealousy, she told Potiphar lies about Joseph to get him into trouble. Poor Joseph was thrown into prison.

But Joseph did not feel alone in prison, because God stayed with him. He made friends among the other prisoners, too.

One day, Joseph heard two other prisoners talking in worried voices. They were Pharaoh's butler and baker, and they had each had a strange dream on the same night.

"I understand a little about dreams," he said. "May I try to help?"

"I dreamed I saw a vine with three branches heavy with ripe grapes," the butler said. "I squeezed the juice from the grapes into Pharaoh's cup."

"That's simple," said Joseph. "In three days, Pharaoh will set you free."

Next, the baker told Joseph his dream.

"I had three baskets of bread for Pharaoh," he said. "But birds swooped out of the sky and ate them all."

"I'm sorry," said Joseph, his heart aching for the man. "In three days, Pharaoh will have you killed."

Everything that Joseph said came true.

Two years later, Pharaoh dreamed that seven fat cows came out of the River Nile. After them came seven thin and bony cows, which ate up the fat cows.

The same night, Pharaoh dreamed of seven healthy ears of corn. Another seven ears of corn sprouted, tiny and shriveled, and swallowed up the healthy corn.

"Who can tell me what these dreams mean?" cried Pharaoh.

Pharaoh's butler suddenly remembered the man in prison who

Pharaoh sent for Joseph and described his dreams to him.

"God is sending you a message," Joseph explained. "Seven years of good harvests are coming, followed by seven years of terrible famine."

Seeing that Joseph was a man of God, Pharaoh freed Joseph and put him in charge of saving Egypt. Joseph became rich and important. He made sure that enough grain was stored up from the good harvests to feed the Egyptian people through the hard years.

Just as Joseph had foreseen, seven years of plenty were followed by terrible famine. People outside of Egypt began to starve. In Canaan, Jacob and his sons were weak and hungry.

"Egypt has plenty of grain," Jacob told his sons. "Surely they can spare some for us?"

So the ten eldest sons set off for Egypt, leaving Benjamin at home.

Joseph was in charge of selling grain to people.

When the brothers reached Egypt, they bowed down before Joseph. Not one of them recognized him.

"It's just like my dream," Joseph thought. "At last I understand God's plan."

"We want to buy some grain," the brothers said.

Joseph hoped that his brothers had changed, and thought of a way to find out. "I think you're spies," he said.

"No, we are all brothers," they cried. "Once there were twelve of us, but one is dead. Our youngest brother is with our father Jacob, in Canaan."

"Bring your youngest brother to me, to prove that your story is true," Joseph said. "Otherwise, I will have you all killed."

He sent the brothers home with sacks of food. But he kept his brother Simeon in Egypt, to make sure that the others would return.

"This is God's punishment for the way we treated Joseph," the brothers whispered to each other.

Tears came to Joseph's eyes when he saw the fear on their faces.

At first, Jacob refused to let Benjamin go to Egypt. Since he had lost Joseph, Benjamin had become Jacob's favorite son, and he didn't want to lose him, even if it meant Simeon would have to stay in Egypt.

But, when they eventually ran out of food, he had to agree.

The brothers returned to Egypt with Benjamin. Joseph released Simeon and invited them all to eat at his house. Then he filled their sacks with food, refusing to accept their money. Secretly, Joseph asked a servant to hide a silver cup in Benjamin's sack of food.

Eventually, the brothers got up to leave.

"Stop!" Joseph yelled. "One of you has stolen my silver cup. Guards, search their sacks!"

When the cup was found in Benjamin's sack, the brothers dropped to their knees in front of Joseph.

"Please, imprison one of us instead," they begged. "Losing Benjamin would break our father's heart."

Joseph listened to them plead for Benjamin's life, and knew for certain that they had changed. Tears rolled down his cheeks as he kneeled down beside his brothers.

"Don't you recognize me?" he whispered.

When Joseph's brothers realized who he was, they couldn't speak for shock and shame. But Joseph smiled at them. He knew that this was all part of God's plan.

"I forgive you," he said.

Trembling, his brothers rose and hugged him. Then Joseph asked them to return to Canaan to tell Jacob the good news.

"Bring your families and all your animals back to Egypt," he said. "I will give you the best land here."

When Jacob heard that Joseph was alive, he could hardly believe it.
It wasn't until he was standing in front of his beloved son that he knew
it was true.

"Father!" cried Joseph, his heart bursting with joy.

They wrapped their arms around each other and wept happy tears.
God had brought them back together at last.

Jacob settled comfortably in Egypt, in the region of Goshen,
and lived to be a great age.